Humphrey's Tiny Tales

My Playful Puppy PROBLEM!

Betty G. Birney worked at Disneyland and the Disney Studios, has written many children's television shows and is the author of over forty books, including the bestselling *The World According to Humphrey*, which won the Richard and Judy Children's Book Club Award, *Friendship According to Humphrey*, *Trouble According to Humphrey*, *Surprises According to Humphrey*, *More Adventures According to Humphrey*, *Holidays According to Humphrey*, *School According to Humphrey*, *Mysteries According to Humphrey* and *Christmas According to Humphrey*. This is the sixth book in her Humphrey's Tiny Tales series. Her work has won many awards, including an Emmy and three Humanitas Prizes. She lives in America with her husband.

Humphrey's Tiny Tales

My Playful Puppy PROBLEM!

BETTY G. BIRNEY

Illustrated by Penny Dann

faber and faber

First published in 2013
by Faber and Faber Limited
Bloomsbury House, 74–77 Great Russell Street,
London WC1B 3DA

Printed in England by CPI Group (UK) Ltd, Croydon, CR0 4YY

The right of Betty G. Birney to be identified
as author of this work has been asserted in accordance
with Section 77 of the Copyright, Designs
and Patents Act 1988

A CIP record for this book
is available from the British Library

ISBN 978–0–571–28247–0

2 4 6 8 10 9 7 5 3 1

Welcome to
MY WORLD

Hi! I'm Humphrey. I'm lucky to be the classroom hamster in Room 26 of Longfellow School. It's a big job because I have to go home with a different student each weekend and try to help my friends. Luckily, my cage has a lock-that-doesn't-lock, so I can get out and have BIG-BIG-BIG adventures!

I'd like you to meet some of my friends

Og

a frog, is the other classroom pet in Room 26. He makes a funny sound: BOING!

Aldo Amato

is a grown-up who cleans Room 26 at night. He's a special friend who always brings me a treat and seems to understand my squeaks better than most humans.

Mrs Brisbane

is our teacher. She really understands her students – even me!

Repeat-It-Please-Richie

is Aldo's nephew and a classmate of mine.

Stop-Giggling-Gail

loves to giggle – and so do I!

Speak-Up-Sayeh

is unsqueakably smart, but she's shy and doesn't like to speak in class.

Raise-Your-Hand-Heidi

is always quick with an answer.

Pay-Attention-Art

is a FUN-FUN-FUN friend!

I think you'll like my other friends, too, such as *Wait-For-The-Bell-Garth, Lower-Your-Voice-A.J. Mrs Brisbane* and *Don't-Complain-Mandy.*

CONTENTS

Pet Project

It was Friday afternoon in Room 26 of Longfellow School, where I'm the classroom hamster.

I was nibbling on a yummy carrot stick when I heard Mrs Brisbane say, 'Class, don't forget to bring in your science projects on Monday.'

That was such exciting news, I almost dropped my carrot.

My classmates had been talking about their experiments all week and they sounded unsqueakably interesting!

I turned to Og, the other classroom pet.

'Did you hear that, Og?' I said. 'We're going to see everyone's science projects on Monday!'

'BOING!' Og replied. He makes a funny sound, but he can't help it. He's a frog.

'Who would like to give us a sneak peek of your project now?' Mrs Brisbane asked.

'I would!' Raise-Your-Hand-Heidi called out.

'Heidi, what did you forget to do?' Mrs Brisbane said.

Heidi raised her hand. 'Sorry,' she said. 'I'm testing different liquids to see how long it takes for them to freeze.'

'Interesting,' Mrs Brisbane said. 'What have you tried?'

'Plain water, sugar water and salt water,' Heidi said.

A.J.'s hand shot up. 'I don't get it,' he said in his loud voice. 'Won't they be melted by the time you get to school?'

'Lower-Your-Voice-A.J.,' Mrs Brisbane reminded him.

'All right,' he said in a softer voice. 'But won't they melt?'

'Yes,' Heidi said. 'So I'm taking pictures and keeping a chart. That's what I'll bring in.' Just thinking about things that are COLD-COLD-COLD made me shiver, even though I have a fur coat!

'How about you, Sayeh?' Mrs Brisbane asked next. Speak-Up-Sayeh didn't raise her hand because she doesn't like to talk in class.

Sayeh smiled shyly. 'I'm growing beans on my windowsill,' she said. 'Some will have full sun and some will be covered.'

Stop-Giggling-Gail was growing mould in her fridge. Mould sounded yucky but Gail said it was fun.

Pay-Attention-Art talked about magnets and Golden-Miranda said something about making a rainbow.

Then I noticed Richie Rinaldi waving his hand.

Mrs Brisbane asked him to speak.

'Mrumsum,' Repeat-It-Please-Richie said. At least that's what *I* heard. And hamsters have very good hearing.

'Repeat-It-Please-Richie,' Mrs Brisbane said. 'And this time, say it so I can understand it.'

'May I take Humphrey home this weekend?' Richie asked. 'I need him for my experiment.'

I was happy to hear that. Classroom pets like me *love* to be needed.

'I thought your project was about

ants,' Mrs Brisbane said.

'It was,' Richie replied. 'But my mum didn't like having ants in the house. Now I have a better idea using a hamster.'

Mrs Brisbane checked her list. 'Yes, Richie,' she said. 'It's your turn to take Humphrey home. Do you want to tell us about your new experiment?'

'Yes, tell us!' I shouted.

Of course, all my friends heard was SQUEAK-SQUEAK-SQUEAK.

Richie thought for a moment. 'I think it should be a surprise.'

Kirk Chen raised his hand. 'I know what it is,' he said. 'Richie's going to turn Humphrey into a monster!'

Then he raised his arms straight up in front of him and made a scary face.

'And when he's a monster, he can have a *ghoul friend*!' Kirk added.

Everybody laughed.

It was funny, unless you were the hamster who was going to be turned into a monster!

And I really didn't want a ghoul friend!

'BOING-BOING-BOING-BOING!' Og sounded unsqueakably worried.

After all, his tank sits next to my cage on the table by the window.

He probably didn't want to have a monster for a neighbour.

But Richie had a big smile on his face.

I was happy for him.

I would have been even happier if I'd known what the experiment was going to be!

'I have a surprise for you at home,' Richie said on the school bus that afternoon.

I slid from one side of my cage to the other because the bus is bumpy and thumpy.

'Just you wait,' Richie said. 'It's a giant surprise.'

A giant is something like a monster. Did Richie already have a giant at home?

'Eeek!' I squeaked.

Richie just laughed. 'You'll find out soon enough,' he said.

The surprise had a name: Poppy.

Poppy was a puppy.

She was small, with curly fur, and she *loved* to bark.

All that barking made my ears twitch and my whiskers wiggle.

'Isn't she great, Humphrey?' Richie asked as he set my cage on the desk in his room. 'I've wanted a dog for years and finally my parents let me have one.'

I didn't really think Poppy was a great pet.

I didn't think *any* dog was great.

Dogs have large, pointed teeth and wet noses.

They have big tails and sharp claws.

And they aren't usually friendly to small creatures like me.

'Woof!' Poppy barked as she tried to jump up and see me.

Luckily, she was too short to get all the way up to my cage.

'She likes you, Humphrey,' Richie laughed. 'She wants to be your friend.'

'Woof!' Poppy barked.

She even wagged her tail.

But I still didn't think she wanted to be my friend.

'Wait until Uncle Aldo comes over tomorrow,' Richie said. 'He's going to help me with my experiment.'

Richie's Uncle Aldo is also our school's cleaner.

At night, when he comes into

Room 26 to clean, he talks to Og and me. Sometimes he balances a broom on one finger and gives us treats.

I was glad I'd be seeing Aldo the next day.

I wasn't
glad about the
experiment, though.

Especially after
we watched a
scary film on
television later
that night.

Richie put my
cage on a high
shelf so Poppy
couldn't get near
me, but that didn't
stop her
from trying.

She looked
up at me

and barked and barked and barked some more.

'WOOF-WOOF! WOOF-WOOF! WOOF-WOOF!'

Richie's mum finally put the puppy in the kitchen so we could watch the film.

It was about a mad scientist called Frankenstein who created a monster. He hooked him up to a scary machine.

There was lightning . . . and the monster came to life.

He had a flat head and bolts sticking out of his neck.

The sight of him made my fur stand up on end!

Richie came over to my cage.

He made weird faces at me and said

'Humphrey-stein' in a creepy voice.

Then he laughed. 'Mwa-ha-ha!'
He didn't sound like Richie at all.

By the time Richie brought me into his room and went to bed, it was raining outside.

Would there be lightning?

Would I end up with bolts in my neck, like Frankenstein's monster?

Would people call me 'Humphrey-stein'?

I crawled into my little sleeping house but I didn't sleep a wink.

I LOVE-LOVE-LOVE being a hamster.

But I would *not* love to be a monster.

I Go for a Spin

During the week, I get to see Aldo every night, but I hardly ever get to see him outside of school.

So I was HAPPY-HAPPY-HAPPY when he came into Richie's room on Saturday afternoon.

'Greetings, my fine furry friend,' Aldo said.

'Glad to see you, Aldo!' I squeaked.

'I think you're glad to see me, too,'
Aldo laughed.

I love to make Aldo laugh because
when he does,
his big, furry
moustache
shakes so
hard, I
sometimes
think it's
going to fall off.

'I hear Richie has planned an
experiment with you,' Aldo said.

I didn't mind if Richie did an
experiment *with* me.

I just didn't want him to do an
experiment *on* me.

'Thanks for helping me, Uncle Aldo,' Richie said.

Just then, Poppy came racing into Richie's room.

'Whoa, slow down, pup,' Aldo told her.

Poppy must not have heard him, because she ran in a circle around his feet.

'Poppy, no!' Aldo said in a firm voice. 'Sit.'

Poppy did not sit.

Instead, she jumped up and put her front paws on Aldo's legs.

'Down, Poppy. Sit down,' Aldo told the dog.

Poppy did not sit down.

She wagged her tail and barked.

'You're going to have to train your dog,' Aldo told Richie.

'I will,' Richie said. 'But she's just a puppy.'

Just then, Poppy noticed me. She raced up to the desk and looked straight at me.

'WOOF-WOOF!' she barked.

'Go away!' I squeaked.

My squeaking only made Poppy bark more.

'Look!' Richie said. 'Poppy wants to play with Humphrey.'

The thought of Poppy playing with me made me shiver and quiver.

Poppy kept on barking. 'WOOF-WOOF-WOOF!'

Her voice was so loud, it made my tiny hamster ears hurt!

Richie's ears must have hurt, too.

He covered them with his hands and shouted, 'Quiet!'

But Poppy was anything but quiet.

'Time for you to go,' Aldo said.

He picked up the little dog and carried her out of the room.

Then he came back in without Poppy and closed the door.

'Now we can get to work,' he said.

'THANKS-THANKS-THANKS, Aldo!' I squeaked.

Aldo said, 'I think Humphrey is glad that Poppy's outside.'

Aldo is a very smart human!

Richie and Aldo pulled chairs up to the desk and looked into my cage.

'HI-HI-HI!' I squeaked.

'So, tell me what you want to do,' Aldo told Richie.

I scrambled to the front of my cage so I could hear Richie's plan.

'I want to see how many times Humphrey can spin his wheel in a minute,' Richie said.

I love spinning on my wheel, so that sounded GREAT-GREAT-GREAT to me.

'That's a good idea,' Aldo said. 'How are you going to do that?'

Richie shrugged. 'I'm not sure. He spins pretty fast. Don't you, Humphrey?'

I scampered over to my wheel and began to spin.

'Hey! Humphrey must have
understood you,' Aldo said.

'But that's impossible,' Richie
replied. 'He's a hamster.'

Aldo laughed. 'You never know
with Humphrey.'

They both leaned in closer as I

began to spin faster and faster.

'I see the problem,' Aldo said. 'He spins so fast, it's hard to count how many times the wheel goes around.'

'Yes,' Richie agreed. 'Should I tell him to slow down?'

Aldo shook his head. 'No. Then it wouldn't be a real experiment.'

I kept on spinning while Richie and Aldo thought about the problem.

Then I heard a distant 'WOOF-WOOF!'

I had almost forgotten about Poppy, but she hadn't forgotten about me.

I heard her scratching at the door and barking.

'Go away, Poppy!' Richie yelled.

I don't think Poppy could hear him over all that barking.

She made me so jumpy, I spun the wheel faster and faster.

'Look at Humphrey go,' Richie said.

'I wish Poppy would go,' I squeaked. 'I wish she'd go far, far away!'

Aldo and Richie watched
me spin on the wheel.

'You need a way to mark
each time the wheel goes
around once,' Aldo said.

 I kept
spinning and
they kept
thinking. I
was hoping
they had an idea soon, because
to squeak the truth, I was
getting tired.

'I know,' Aldo said. 'We need something that makes a sound.'

Whew! I was GLAD-GLAD-GLAD that Aldo had come up with an idea.

I let my wheel slow down a bit while I tried to think of something that makes a sound.

Luckily, Poppy wasn't making any sounds outside the door.

I looked over at the side of the cage where my water bottle and food dish are.

Sometimes my water bottle makes a GLUG-GLUG-GLUG sound.

But it's not very loud.

I looked over at my poo corner —
no sound there!

I looked down at my soft bedding.
It was nice and quiet.

Then I
looked up and
saw a tiny
little bell.

Not long
ago, my friends gave it to me for a
surprise.

I stopped spinning and hopped off
my wheel.

Then I scampered up to the top of
my cage and rang the little bell with
my paw.

DING-
DING-DING!
Aldo and
Richie were so
busy thinking,
they didn't hear
it.

I tried again.
DING-DING-
DING-DING!
This time,
Aldo looked up.
'What's that
sound?' he
asked.
Richie looked
up, too.

'Oh, that's Humphrey's new bell,' he said.

Aldo leaned in close to my cage. 'A bell? That's just what we need! Thanks, Humphrey!'

'You're unsqueakably welcome,' I told him.

Aldo probably didn't understand my squeaks, but I was happy he liked my idea.

Then Richie and Aldo went to work.

First, Richie took my wheel out of the cage and put it on the desk.

'Don't worry, Humphrey,' he said. 'You'll get it back.'

Aldo made a stand out of a coat hanger.

He hung the bell on the coat hanger with a piece of string and set it near the wheel.

'We need something that will ring the bell each time the wheel spins,' Aldo said. 'It must be strong enough to ring the bell but small enough to fit under the wheel.'

This time, Richie came up with a good idea.

Soon, they had attached a bent paper clip to the side of my wheel.

'Humphrey, we need your help again,' Richie said.

That was GOOD-GOOD-GOOD news, because classroom hamsters like me love to help!

Richie reached into my cage and gently placed me on my wheel again.

'You know what to do, Humphrey,' he said.

Yes, I did!

I began to spin my wheel, faster and faster.

DING-DING-DING-DING-DING!

Just then, Richie put his hand on my wheel.

I stopped so suddenly, I tumbled over.

'Sorry, Humphrey,' he said.

As he gently placed me back in my cage, Richie told me, 'I need to finish the rest of the experiment.'

The *rest* of the experiment?

What was coming next?

Would I end up like the monster in the Frankenstein film?

Just then, I heard something whining and scratching at the door.

Poppy was back!

'WOOF-WOOF!' she barked.

I shivered a little.

I didn't want to turn into a monster.

And I REALLY-REALLY-REALLY didn't want to play with Poppy!

The Great Dog
Disaster

'I know what puppies like,' Aldo said.
'I'll take Poppy out in the garden
and we'll play with her ball.'

Aldo is an unsqueakably nice man!

Things were quiet while Aldo and
Poppy were gone.

Richie quietly drew a chart
and began decorating a big board
describing his experiment.

'Poppy loves fetching that ball,'
Aldo said when he came back. 'I left
her in the garden for a while.'

That was GOOD-GOOD-GOOD
news!

Aldo gave Richie a stopwatch, so
he could time my spinning.

'Are you ready, Humphrey?' Richie asked.

He gently took me out of my cage and set me on the wheel.

I started spinning, slowly at first.

Then I picked up speed.

'Ready, set, go!' Richie said as he started the stopwatch.

I spun faster and faster.

DING-DING!

Each time the bell rang, Richie made a mark on his chart.

DING-DING-DING!

I picked up speed.

'Go, Humphrey!' Aldo said.

DING-DING-DING-DING!

I spun so fast, Richie had trouble keeping up.

'That's one minute,' Richie said. 'Keep going, Humphrey.'

I can spin on my wheel for a long time.

And I liked the sound of the bell ringing.

Aldo took pictures of me.

'Smile, Humphrey!' he said as a bright light flashed.

'Two minutes,' Richie announced.

I kept on spinning and spinning.

After all, I wanted Richie to get good marks for his experiment.

I lost track of how many minutes I spun.

'That's it,' Richie said after a while. 'You can rest now, Humphrey.'

He slowed the wheel with his hand and then moved me back to my cage.

'I think Humphrey needs a nap,' Aldo said.

He was right about that!

'And I have to get home,' Aldo added. 'I don't think you need my help any more.'

As Richie said goodbye to Aldo, I burrowed under my soft bedding and fell asleep.

When I woke up, Richie was sitting at his desk, writing his report.

'How's it going?' I squeaked.

'Hi, Humphrey,' he said. 'You did a lot of spinning today.'

'I'm always happy to help,' I said.

And I REALLY-REALLY-REALLY meant it.

Later, when Richie went to bed, his mum and dad came in to say goodnight.

'Will you be able to finish the project tomorrow?' his dad asked.

'Yes,' Richie said with a smile. 'I'm

almost finished now.'

When they left the room, his parents turned out the lights and shut the door.

But it wasn't long before I heard someone scratching and whining outside.

It was Poppy!

'Sometimes she sleeps in my room, Humphrey,' Richie said. 'But I think I should keep her away from you.'

'*Far* away!' I agreed.

Luckily, I heard Richie's mum say, 'No, Poppy. You'll sleep in our room tonight.'

And then, finally, it was quiet.

I slept well that night and so did Richie.

On Sunday, Richie did the last bits of his project.

By late afternoon, the report, the chart and the photos were up on the board.

Richie had used bright colours and
it looked GREAT-GREAT-GREAT!
My wheel with the bell and the
clip sat in front of the big board.

'You did a hamster-iffic job!' I squeaked to Richie.

'It turned out pretty well,' Richie said. 'I just hope Mrs Brisbane likes it.'

'She will!' I told him and I meant it.

Once in a while, I'd hear Poppy scratching at the door.

Sometimes, she even barked.

'WOOF-WOOF!'

But Richie kept the door tightly closed, which made me unsqueakably happy!

When he was finished, Richie's whole family came in to see the project.

Richie put me on the wheel and I start spinning as fast as I could while he explained how it worked.

His two sisters and his brother were so excited to see me spin, I went even faster.

'Go, Humphrey, go!' they shouted.

When Richie made me stop spinning, his mum said, 'I'm proud of you, Richie.'

'I'm proud of you *and* Humphrey,' his dad said. 'Let's celebrate and go out for supper.'

'Sounds like fun!' I squeaked.

But it turns out that hamsters aren't allowed in restaurants.

Not even neat and polite hamsters like me.

Soon, I was alone in Richie's room. The house was quiet and I dozed off.

I'm not sure how long I was asleep before I heard a whining sound.

Poppy was outside Richie's bedroom door!

Luckily the door was closed.

I closed my eyes and tried to get back to sleep.

Then I heard a scratching sound.

'WOOF-WOOF!' Poppy barked.

The noise got louder and louder and the door began to shake.

I'm not sure what Poppy did, but suddenly, the door burst open and there she was!

She didn't waste any time.
She ran straight towards the desk,
jumped up on Richie's chair and
looked at me.

I had never been so happy to live in a cage!

But if Poppy could open the door to the room, could she also open the door to my cage?

She might figure out that my cage has a lock-that-doesn't-lock.

My heart was pounding.

'Stay away!' I squeaked. 'I don't want to play.'

'WOOF-WOOF!' she answered, wagging her tail.

Poppy put her front legs up on the top of the desk to try to get closer.

Suddenly there was a loud crash as her big puppy paws sent the wheel sliding across the desk.

The big board collapsed.

The bell went DING-DING-DING.

Luckily, the noise scared Poppy.

She jumped off the chair and ran out of the room.

I was HAPPY-HAPPY-HAPPY that she was gone.

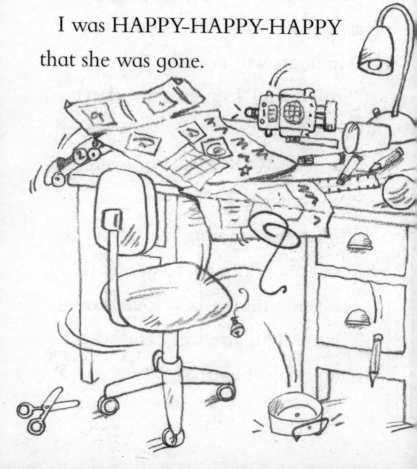

But I was SORRY-SORRY-SORRY when I looked at the desk.

The pieces of Richie's project were scattered everywhere.

It was completely ruined!

And all because of that playful puppy.

'Oh, no!' Richie shouted when he returned.

His mum and dad ran into the room.

'What could have happened?' Mrs Rinaldi said.

Mr Rinaldi looked around the room.

'Richie, was the door open when

you got back?' he asked. 'Because I remember closing it before we left so Poppy couldn't get in.'

'Yes, it was,' Richie said. 'So I guess she must have done it.'

'YES-YES-YES!' I squeaked. 'Poppy came in and wrecked the project!'

Just then, the puppy raced into the room.

'Bad dog!' Richie said.

Poppy just wagged her tail.

'She's just a puppy,' Richie's mum reminded him. 'She didn't know what she was doing.'

I wasn't so sure.

Mrs Rinaldi took Poppy out of the

room and closed the door.

Richie and Mr Rinaldi sat down and tried to put the project back together.

The board was torn, so Richie taped it back together.

He smoothed out his wrinkled report.

'What happened to the bell?'
Richie asked.

His dad began to search for it.

'And where's the clip?' Richie
wondered.

He began to search for it.

They spent a LONG-LONG-
LONG time looking for the missing
pieces.

Richie looked on the floor.

Mr Rinaldi looked on the desk.

'The clip slid under the lamp!' I
shouted. 'And the bell is under the
desk.'

'It's getting late,' Mrs Rinaldi said
when she came back into the room.

Luckily, Poppy wasn't with her.

'I've got to fix my project tonight,'
Richie said. 'It's due tomorrow!'

Mrs Rinaldi joined the search.

Finally, Richie crawled under the
desk. 'Here's the bell!'

'And here's the clip,' his mum said
as she lifted up the lamp.

I felt a lot better and so did Richie.

But when he tried to put the project back together, it didn't work.

He placed me on the wheel and I began to spin.

When the bell hit the clip, the bell fell off.

Instead of going 'DING', it went 'CLUNK'.

He worked on it some more.

This time, when the bell hit the clip, the clip fell off.

'Oh, I can't do anything right,' Richie said.

Richie's dad tried to help.

When he finished, the bell didn't fall off, but it didn't ring at all.

'Richie needs to get to bed,' Mrs Rinaldi said. 'Now.'

'I'm sure you can fix it in the morning, son,' Mr Rinaldi said. 'We all need some sleep.'

I know Richie didn't want to go to bed, but soon he was fast asleep.

I, however, was wide awake.

The moon glowed brightly that night and I could see the wheel from my cage.

I stared and stared at it all night long.

It was almost morning when I saw the problem.

Mr Rinaldi had fastened the bell too tightly.

Someone needed to loosen the string that held it onto the hanger.

And I was the only someone who knew what to do.

The Playful Puppy Returns

There was no time to waste!

I jiggled the lock-that-doesn't-lock on my cage.

The door swung open.

I was about to scurry over to the wheel to repair the bell, when Richie's mum knocked on the door.

'Richie! Time to get up!' she called out.

I hurried back to my cage as fast as my small legs would carry me.

After all, if I ever get caught outside my cage, someone might fix my lock-that-doesn't-lock.

Then, I could never get out and help my friends again.

Just as I closed the door, Richie jumped out of bed.

He yawned and said, 'Hi, Humphrey.'

I squeaked back politely as he came over to look at the wheel.

'I wish I could get that bell to ring,' he said.

His mum called from the hall. 'Come and have your breakfast, Richie. You're going to be late!'

'But I want to fix my project,' he replied.

'You have to eat first,' she said.

Richie sighed and left his room.

I knew if he was eating breakfast, he'd be gone for a while, so I opened the door to my cage again and hurried over to the wheel.

It wouldn't take long for me to loosen the string so the bell would ring.

Suddenly, I heard the pitter-patter of paws on the floor.

I looked up and saw that Richie had left the door open.

Poppy was heading straight towards the desk!

She whined and wagged her tail as she looked up at me.

'Go away, Poppy!' I squeaked.

She hopped up on the chair and stared at me across the desk.

I could see her shiny teeth, and this time I didn't have my cosy cage to protect me.

I glanced around and saw a pile of paper clips on the desk.

I threw them at her nose, hoping to chase her away.

Poppy growled, but she didn't move.

Then I remembered that Aldo had said that she liked playing with a ball.

I'd seen a little bouncy ball on Richie's desk.

I scurried to it and rolled it towards the edge.

'Here, Poppy – catch!' I squeaked.

The ball rolled off the desk and across the floor.

While the pup chased after it, I worked on loosening the string.

To my surprise, Poppy came right back with the ball in her mouth.

She hopped up on the chair and set

the ball on the desk.

'WOOF-WOOF!' she barked.

Poppy still wanted to play.

I took a quick look around the desk and grabbed a small ruler.

Using the ruler like a bat, I swung it and hit the ball hard.

This time, the ball rolled much further away and Poppy chased after it.

I worked fast to loosen the string, but the pup came right back again and set the ball on the desk again.

'WOOF-WOOF!' she barked.

Her shiny white teeth looked SHARP-SHARP-SHARP.

I picked up the ruler again and aimed it in a different direction.

I gave it good hard whack and the ball flew off the desk and rolled under Richie's bed!

I heard Poppy's paws racing across the floor, but I didn't stop to watch her.

Instead, I stood up on my back paws and gave the string a good tug with my front paws.

Then I gave the wheel a spin and when the bell hit the clip, it rang.

DING–DING–DING!

It worked!

I raced back to my cage and closed the door behind me, just as Poppy returned with the ball.

'Sorry, Poppy. I don't want to play catch any more,' I squeaked.

It wasn't long before Richie came back to his room and got dressed.

'Richie! We're about to leave for school!' Richie's dad called to him. 'Get your project together.'

'What's the point?' Richie said. 'It doesn't work. Mrs Brisbane will give me a bad mark.'

'Try it!' I squeaked.

Richie walked over to the desk and looked down at my wheel.

'I don't understand why it doesn't ring,' he said.

Then he gave the wheel a spin and the bell hit the clip.

DING!

'I don't believe it,' Richie said.

He spun the wheel again.

DING!

'It works!' Richie grinned, giving the wheel another spin.

DING!

'I don't know what happened,' he said. 'But I'm glad it's fixed now.'

Richie wasn't the only one who was GLAD-GLAD-GLAD!

Once we got to school, Richie and all the other students in Room 26 set up their projects.

'Og, you're not going to believe what happened,' I told my froggy friend.

'BOING-BOING!' he answered.

Og sounded concerned, so I said, 'Don't worry, Og. It turned out well in the end.'

Then Mrs Brisbane asked my friends to explain their science projects.

It was unsqueakably interesting to learn from Heidi that plain water froze faster than sugar water. And the salt water didn't freeze at all!

Sayeh showed us the beans she'd grown.

The beans that had received the most light grew the best.

And the colourful mould that
Gail had grown in her fridge was
amazing!

Finally, it was Richie's turn.

He explained his experiment to the
class.

Then, he took me out of my cage
and placed me on my wheel.

'Why don't we all get a little closer

so we can watch?' Mrs Brisbane said.

I was HAPPY-HAPPY-HAPPY to start spinning.

DING-DING-DING!

The bell rang every single time the wheel went around.

DING-DING-DING-DING!

'Look at him go!' Lower-Your-Voice-A.J. shouted.

Golden-Miranda cheered me on, too. 'Faster, Humphrey, faster!'

'I think Humphrey needs a rest,' Mrs Brisbane said. 'But you've done a wonderful job, Richie!'

As the wheel slowed down, I looked up at Richie.

He had a huge smile on his face.

I think I had a huge smile on my face, too.

(Some humans think that hamsters don't smile, but we do.)

'Good job,' Kirk told Richie. 'But I still think you should have turned Humphrey into a monster!'

I like Kirk a lot, but I didn't agree with him.

I just want to be a helpful classroom hamster who goes home with my classmates at the weekend.

I love going home with my friends. *Even* friends who have very playful puppies!

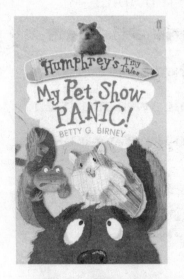

Humphrey's *Tiny Tales*

My Pet Show
PANIC!

BETTY G. BIRNEY

Humphrey's *Tiny Tales*

My Summer Fair
SURPRISE!

BETTY G. BIRNEY

Humphrey's *Tiny Tales*

My Creepy-Crawly Camping
ADVENTURE!

BETTY G. BIRNEY

Humphrey's *Tiny Tales*

My Great Big
BIRTHDAY BASH!

BETTY G. BIRNEY

Have you read all my tiny tales?

See what unsqueakably exciting adventures I've had . .

Humphrey and his friends have been hard at work making a brand new FUN-FUN-FUN website just for you!

Play Humphrey's exciting new game, share your pet pictures, find fun crafts and activities, read Humphrey's very own diary and discover all the latest news from your favourite furry friend at:

www.funwithhumphrey.com